Bumble and Bee

Don't Worry, BEE Happy

ROSS BURACH

ACORN™
SCHOLASTIC INC.

To Sophie and Henry — RB

Library of Congress Cataloging-in-Publication Data
Names: Burach, Ross, author, illustrator.
Title: Don't worry, bee happy / Ross Burach.
Description: First edition. | New York : Acorn/Scholastic Inc., 2020. |
Series: Bumble and Bee ; book 1 | Audience: Ages 4-6. | Audience: Grades K-1. |
Summary: Whether it is best friends picture day or the waggle dance, Bumble and Bee buzz around the pond,
trying to engage Froggy in their playful activities—even coming up with a terrifying way to cure Froggy's hiccups.
Identifiers: LCCN 2019027463 (print) | LCCN 2019027464 (ebook) | ISBN 9781338504927 (v. 1 ; paperback) |
ISBN 9781338504934 (v. 1 ; hardback) | ISBN 9781338504941 (v. 1 ; ebk)
Subjects: LCSH: Bumblebees–Juvenile fiction. | Bees–Juvenile fiction. | Frogs–Juvenile fiction. |
Best friends–Juvenile fiction. | Hiccups–Juvenile fiction. | Humorous stories. | CYAC: Bumblebees–Fiction. | Bees–
Fiction. | Frogs–Fiction. | Best friends–Fiction. | Friendship–Fiction. | Humorous stories. | LCGFT: Humorous fiction.
Classification: LCC PZ7.1.B868 Do 2020 (print) | LCC PZ7.1.B868 (ebook) | DDC (E)–dc23

10 9 8 7 6 5 4 3 2 1   20 21 22 23 24
Printed in China   62
First edition, January 2020
Book design by Marijka Kostiw
Edited by Tracy Mack

Best Friends Picture Day

Click

3

6

Let's try this again.
On three, say, **BEES!**

1 . . .
2 . . .
3 . . .

BEES!
Click

8

9

11

A Bad Case
of the Hiccups

Squirt

Honey

Poor Froggy has a bad case of the hiccups.

:Hiccup:

We must help our friend. But how?

We will scare the hiccups out of Froggy.

Froggy will be so HAPPY!

How do we scare Froggy?

By using the element of . . .

SURPRISE!

AHHHHH

But first, we have to ask what Froggy is scared of.

Hiccup

(17)

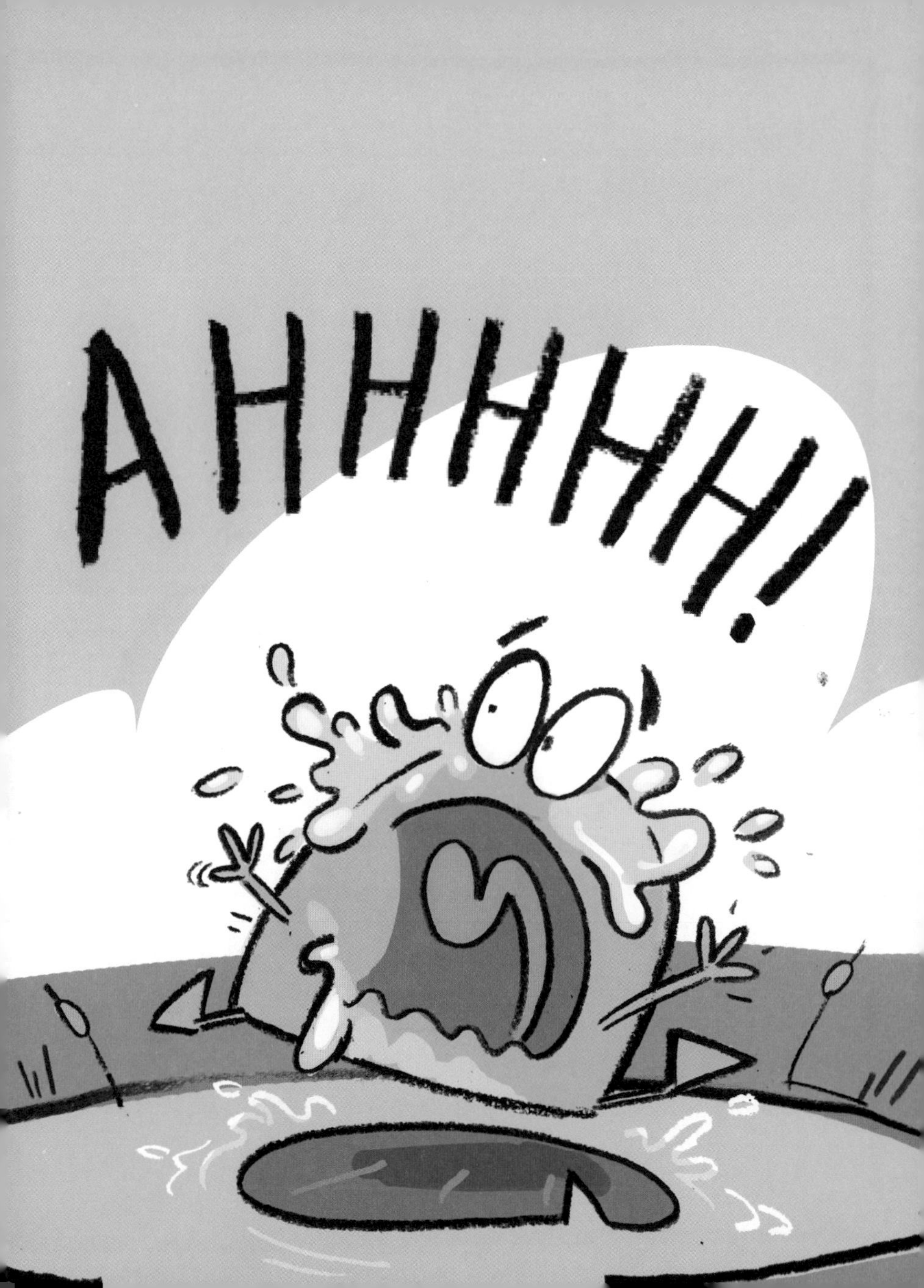
AHHHHHH!

The Waggle Dance

28

Do a figure eight!

Nectar is in sight!

31

32

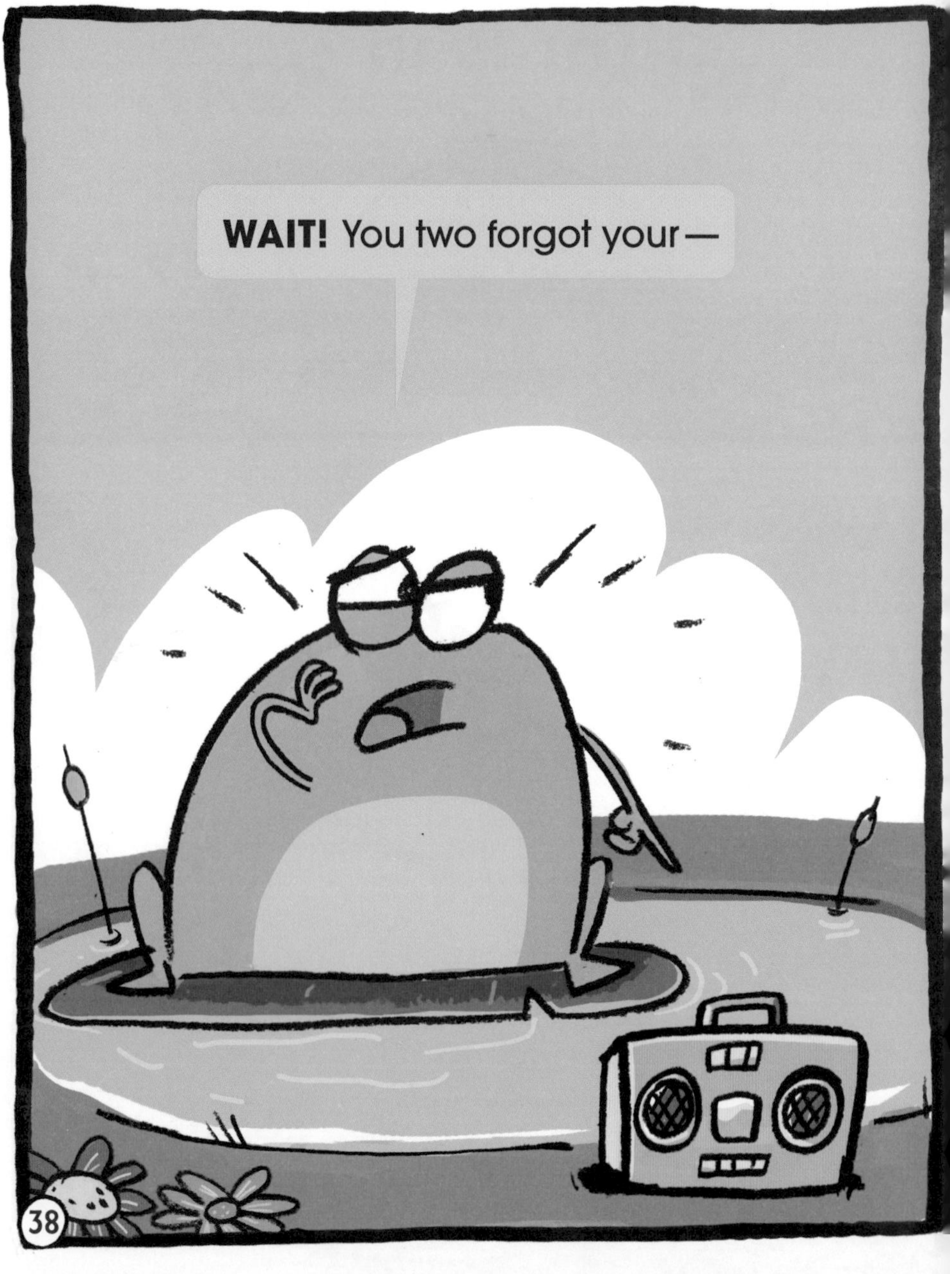
WAIT! You two forgot your—

PLAY

39

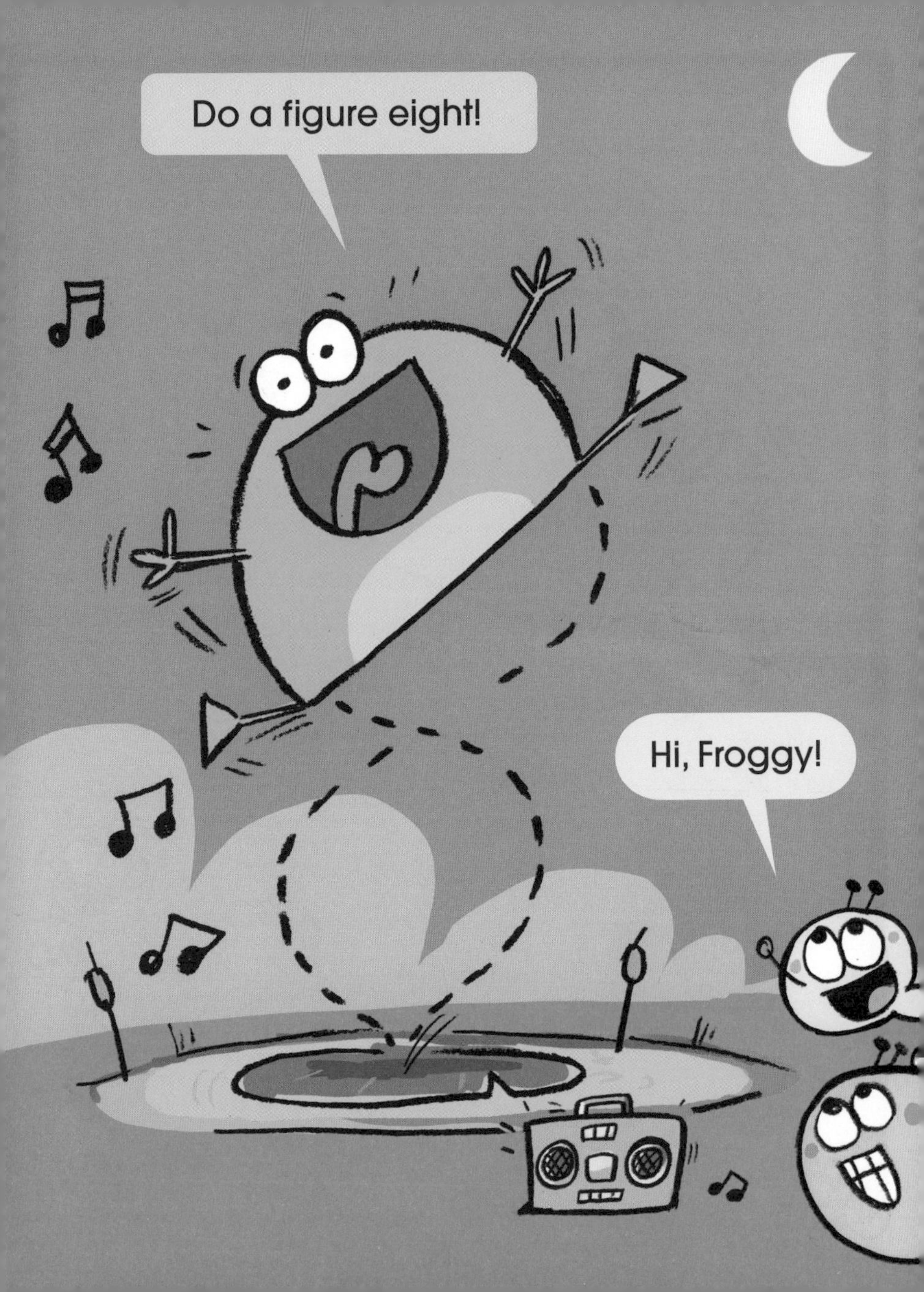
Do a figure eight!
Hi, Froggy!

ker-ploosh!

44

About the Author

Ross Burach lives with his family in Brooklyn, New York, where he spends his days drawing bees and frogs, and doing waggle dances. He is the creator of the very funny picture books **The Very Impatient Caterpillar** and **Truck Full of Ducks**, as well as the board books **Potty All-Star** and **Hi-Five Animals!**, named the best board book of the year by **Parents** magazine. Bumble and Bee is Ross's first early reader series.

YOU CAN DRAW FROGGY!

Make me look good.

1 To make Froggy's body, draw a closed half oval.

2 To make the eyes, draw two circles, a line through both, and two small dots.

3 Add a frown! To make the arms, draw four lines.

4 To make the fingers, draw three joined U's at the bottom of each arm.

5 To make the legs, draw a curved line on each side of Froggy, and two small triangle feet. Add a lily pad.

6 Color in your drawing!

Nice work.

WHAT'S YOUR STORY?

Bumble and Bee are doing a waggle dance!
What is **your** favorite kind of dance?
Who do you like to dance with?
What kind of music will you play?
Write and draw your story!